Beans and Lolo
Bike the Heartland

Written by
R. J. Kinderman

Illustrated by
Mary Waterfall

follow your dreams

SPINNING WHEELS PUBLISHING

Publisher's Cataloging-in-Publication
(Provided by Quality Books, Inc.)

Kinderman, R. J.
    Beans and Lolo bike the heartland / written by R.J. Kinderman ; illustrated by Mary Waterfall.
       pages cm
    SUMMARY: In this rhyming story, two children bike middle America in an exciting, educational journey highlighting unique geography, people, and favorite pastimes. Audience: Grades K-3.
       ISBN 978-0-9856469-4-3
       1. Bicycle touring--Middle West--Juvenile fiction. 2. Middle West--Description and travel--Juvenile fiction. 3. Stories in rhyme. [1. Bicycle touring--Fiction. 2. Middle West--Description and travel--Fiction. 3. Stories in rhyme.]   I. Waterfall, Mary, illustrator. II. Title.

PZ8.3.K5655Beb 2016   [E]
                                       QBI16-600023

Interior and cover/dust jacket layout by Heather McElwain, Turtle Bay Creative

    Special thanks to the Green Bay Packers and Jerry Hanson; Cheeseheads and Ralph Bruno; Indycar Licensing and Bill Smith; and RAGBRAI and Scott Garner for allowing me to include illustrations of these businesses in *Beans and Lolo Bike the Heartland.* I hope that these organizations enjoy the child-friendly representations of their businesses in this book as much as children do.   —RJK

Printed in China

To Denise
and all other Super Grandmas
everywhere.
—RJK

Thanks to Mom and Dad
for their support and encouragement
in all my creative endeavors as a kid.
—Mary Waterfall

**Beans and Lolo biked America from sea to shining sea,
but in between two oceans, they had much more to see.**

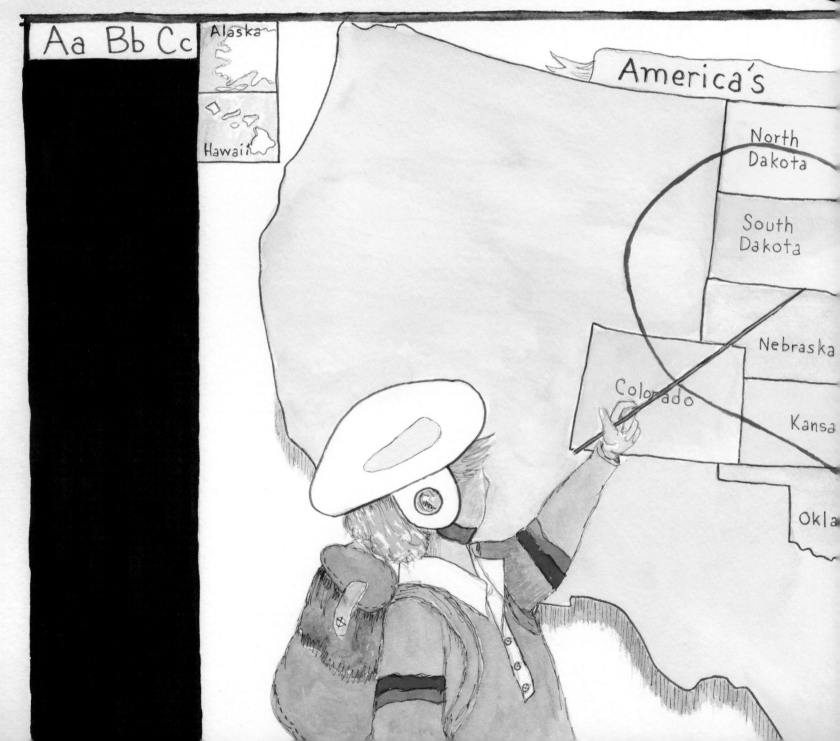

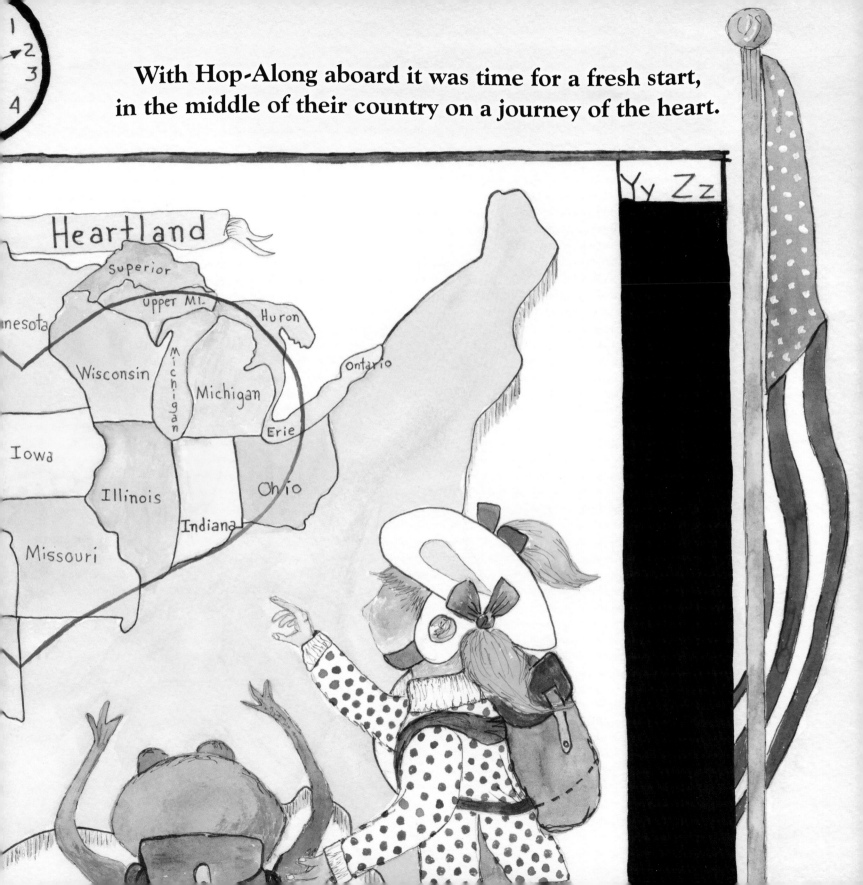

**With Hop-Along aboard it was time for a fresh start,
in the middle of their country on a journey of the heart.**

Beans and Lolo loved the U.P.
and the Yoopers living there.
They were smitten with the mitten,
and the Great Lakes everywhere.

The birthplace of eight presidents,
astronauts, and Orville Wright,
and Ohio's Thomas Edison
helped the bikers see at night.

OHIO
Birthplace of Presidents
and
Aviation Pioneers

Where basketball is worshipped,
you'll find Hoosiers full of pride.
Hop-Along drove a race car
for a fast and scary ride.

They biked through a windy city
on Lake Michigan's southwest shore.
They pedaled the land of Lincoln,
a naval base, and more.

Through miles and miles of corn, under a blue and sun-filled sky,
rolled 15,000 riders on a journey named RAGBRAI.

Beans ate watermelon and pork chops, Lolo ate turkey legs and pie.
And on every road along the way, people waved and shouted "Hi!"

With a silver rainbow in the sky, at the gateway to the west,
Beans and Lolo saw for themselves that the Show-Me state was best.

In a state with a panhandle, Beans and Lolo got their kicks,
rolling down a much-loved highway with the name Route 66.

Sheep and cattle watched the three friends
as they biked across the plains.
Strong cowboys riding bucking bulls
walked away with aches and pains.

High up in the mountains
in a cold and freezing breeze,
Lolo surfed a half-pipe
while Beans and Hop-Along rode skis.

Sunflowers filled the prairies
and dark clouds piled high,
as a twister caught the friends
and Lolo cried out, "Oh my!"

"We're not in Kansas anymore,"
cried Beans from way up high.
Chimney Rock pierced the clouds
as Hop-Along raced quickly by.

NEBRASKA
...the
good life

From the Badlands to the Black Hills,
as is every camper's dream,
Beans and Lolo panned for gold
beside a rippling stream.

Black Hills Gold
South Dakota

Through oceans of wheat and oil fields,
Beans and Lolo biked all day.
From grains for bread to gas for cars,
this state feeds the USA.

In the Boundary Waters Wilderness,
they saw wolves, and moose, and more.
They passed a lighthouse and a lift bridge
as they biked the great north shore.

The Mississippi blocked the buddies
who didn't have a boat,
so Beans and Lolo rode a water bike,
and Hop-Along backstroked.

Rolling through America's Dairyland, eating cheese on crispy crackers,
Beans and Lolo stopped to tailgate and cheer on the Green Bay Packers.

Aboard the Lake Michigan ferry with the lake as smooth as cream,
the three friends drifted off to sleep, seeing far-off places in their dreams.

Lolo dreamed of visiting Eskimos who call Alaska home,
where a team of sled dogs saved the day bringing medicine to Nome.

She dreamed of polar bears and glaciers, and all the other sights.
Would they even fall asleep beneath bright northern lights?

Beans dreamed of where brave sailors fought to keep our country free.
Would they watch volcanoes explode, and lava flowing to the sea?

He dreamed of rainbow-colored fish out in the deep blue sea.
Would they surf or paddle outriggers or sleep beneath palm trees?

The three friends' eyes popped open:
It all had seemed so real.
There were no pretty colored fish,
no Eskimos, or seals.

As the ferry pulled up to the dock
and the bikers rode ashore,
they were back where they had started
greeting family, friends, and more.

Looking back upon their trip, they tried to pick a favorite part.

They found it was impossible on a journey of the heart.

With two bike trips behind them, Beans and Lolo wanted more.
Who knows what might await them far across some distant shore?